Dead Devil's Night

MAREE ROSE

Dead Devil's Night

by Maree Rose

Cover Art by Maree Rose

Blurb

ONE NIGHT.

That was all it took for Rylan's world to disappear.

A year has passed, filled with plotting.

Because this year, on that one night, she will make them pay.

THIS DEAD DEVIL'S NIGHT, SHE WILL GIVE THEM THEIR OWN INTRODUCTION TO HELL.

Foreword

Hello readers!

Thank you so much for choosing up my book!

Please be aware that this book is a MFM romance, meaning our leading lady Rylan will not have to choose between her men, because #whychoose.

Warning, this book is a dark contemporary romance. It contains very explicit 18+ dark, sexual content, and straight-up smut.

There are no heroes here, only characters with psycho tendencies and therefore there is unaliving people, and lots of dark and twisted content.

All the characters are 18+

Please proceed at your own risk.

Thank you and I hope you enjoy Dead Devil's Night.

MAREE ROSE

Content Warnings

If you don't have any triggers and feel like taking a gamble on the content then just skip the next page completely.

For those who do need to check the warnings then they are listed on the next page for your reference.

 Warnings

I know we all love a shopping list of warnings and I usually love giving them to you. However, this is a short novella and therefore there aren't too many warnings to be had.

In saying that there is a big blaring warning right from the get go.

There is r@pe/SA and v!olence in the prologue.

It is not detailed but it is there and does set the scene for the whole story.

From then on it is a very dark revenge story with a LOT of v!olence and detailed unaliving.

For everyone who has dreamt of a
blood soaked revenge, I got you!

Prologue

T raumatic experiences are always unique to the individual experiencing them. There is no gauge for how something will affect a person.

Watching my best friends slowly bleed out from multiple stab wounds as they are forced to watch a group of men rape me and then stab me can absolutely cause lasting trauma.

I had grown up with the twins, Rev and Kai. From the moment the authorities threw me into the foster home, they took me under their wing. We had been inseparable since that day twelve years ago.

They had been there to cheer on my successes, wrap me up in their arms when I was sad, and beat the shit out of the guys that turned into assholes and cheated on me in high school. And then they were also there to watch me die.

When the twins aged out of the system, they found an abandoned apartment building and created a home out of the ruined remains on one of the upper floors. For the two years after that, while I was still at the foster home, I spent all available free time there. What I could steal from the foster home without it being noticed, I did.

And when the time came, there was a room waiting for me.

For four years after the day I turned eighteen, we had each done what we could to provide for our family. We took jobs wherever we could to put food on the table and buy whatever we needed to survive.

They were my everything.

We respected the space we had created and kept all of our sexual encounters far away from our home. Or, at least, the few attempts I had made to find someone I did. But every one night stand always felt wrong, so it wasn't long before I stopped looking. Because in the end those men weren't the two men I lived with.

If the twins still looked, they never flaunted any of their encounters and never spoke of their conquests.

They were even at the bar with me the last few times I tried to meet someone. After my dates abandoned me when my back was turned, they would walk me home.

We were like any normal family, coming and going depending on our work or whatever else we were doing. But we always made sure to have at least one night dedicated to being together, cooking, eating and watching a movie until we fell asleep.

And every year on Dead Devil's night, without fail, we locked ourselves within the safety of our home together. We played board games by candlelight and ate the worst food we could get our hands on. It was our own Dead Devil's tradition.

We had an entire night planned, as we did every year on that night. The night everyone called Dead Devil's night. It was the one night of the year where there was no law. The crazies come out of the woodwork and terrorize the streets, killing and causing utter chaos to anyone stupid enough to not stay behind locked doors.

I had the day off my bike courier job, so I had spent the morning cleaning the apartment and dyeing my hair a pretty violet color. While the twins chose to decorate their bodies with tattoos, I chose to change my hair color. I had chosen some pretty extreme colors in the past, but the violet became my favorite and seemed to make my dark blue eyes pop.

We had spent the afternoon cooking a light meal and then gathering our junk food and supplies for our tradition. As usual, Kai teased me about my hair color, but I could tell he secretly liked it with the amount of times he played with it. Rev, on the other hand, just kissed my forehead and then smacked my ass in his effort to get me out of the kitchen.

It wasn't long after the sun had set that the noises started.

My heart sped up. They seemed louder than normal, closer.

Rev and Kai were sitting on either side of me as our laughter and happiness sputtered out at the sounds of screams and howling. The sound of shattered glass came from the street below, and Rev quickly got up to look out the window at the street below.

I could see the moment his jaw clenched, his tattooed hands gripping the longer parts of his black hair before he turned back towards us. He came over and started blowing out the candles, Kai quickly hopping up to help.

The building we were in wasn't in the heart of the city where all the chaos normally happened. They didn't normally come out this far. Rev and Kai said they had chosen it to keep me safe and away from the potential darkness people had to embrace to live in the cesspit at the center.

What happened next was the stuff of nightmares. A person could wonder whether the light in our window was what drew their attention, or if it was when the candles were blown out that caught their eyes.

The boys had gone to retrieve the bats they kept in their bedrooms as protection, but it was already too late.

Their bats did not stand a chance against the five men who broke down our door wielding spiked bats, knives and other weapons. The small amount of self defense training that the boys had taught me was useless.

The men took their time taunting the twins, tying them up and stabbing them before positioning them on their stomachs with their faces held in a position to see me.

They had to watch while each of the men forced themselves on me, stabbing me with both dicks and knives until I could no longer scream. Until I could no longer feel anything.

My head was turned toward them, watching the tears and blood flow from them in utter devastation and pain.

The blackness had started to eat away at my vision as the last man forced himself between my legs.

I couldn't fight anymore. I couldn't scream. I couldn't make any sounds.

I was screaming on the inside. I was trapped in a nightmare that I wasn't going to escape from.

It was even a struggle to keep focusing on the twins' faces.

I just wanted to sleep. I was so cold, the chill of the night was sinking into my bones.

Rev's eyes started to lose focus, his blinks becoming longer and more drawn out. Kai's face twitched as he tried again to fight against the ropes, but he slumped again after only a second, the effort doing more harm than good.

Blinking my eyes became harder, and between one blink and the next, I watched as Kai's eyes shut, not opening again.

When my eyes closed the next time, they wouldn't open again. The blackness was all-encompassing.

I couldn't see. I couldn't feel. I couldn't survive.

Chapter 1

Rylan

12 Months Later

The dreams always came every night without fail. They were never about the attack itself. in some ways, it would have been easier if they were. Instead, other memories haunted me, happy memories of times I had spent with Rev and Kai before the attack. And that made it far worse.

I was walking back toward the bar after needing to use the ladies room when I noticed that my date was no longer where I left him. Instead there was someone else far more familiar. Sliding back onto the barstool, I quirked an eyebrow. "Where is Matt?"

Kai flashed me a grin. "I saw him as he went out the exit. Seemed like he was in a rush."

I huffed in response. "Did you scare away my date?"

He chuckled, picking up the glass of bourbon in front of him and then tapping it against the matching drink in front of me. "I didn't do anything, gorgeous. Drink up, and I'll walk you home."

It wasn't the first time this exact scenario occurred, which was why I asked the question. I knew they felt protective of me, but lately it was like their protective nature was in overdrive.

Picking up the glass, I knocked it back in one swallow, expecting to cringe at the harshness but finding myself pleasantly surprised. He had somehow scored a decent quality from the bartender. Grinning at the look on my face, he swallowed his own drink and gestured for me to walk ahead of him.

"Luckily there aren't that many people here or I may have had to make a scene poking out a few eyes for seeing you in this outfit."

I rolled my eyes, but when I looked over my shoulder at him, he was just scowling in the direction of the two other patrons in the bar. When his eyes returned to mine, he just grinned as though he wasn't doing anything wrong and then took bigger steps to catch up again as we exited the bar.

He tugged on a strand of my hair when he's beside me. "Have I told you red is my new favorite color?"

I laughed at his absurdity and shoved a hand into his side, pushing him away as he continued to grin at me. I dyed my hair a cherry apple red only that morning for my date. Matched with the one simple black dress that I owned and red lipstick, I thought I looked pretty hot. And I had gotten the impression that Matt thought so too, but I guess I was wrong.

Suddenly an arm landed across my shoulders, and I tensed up momentarily until the familiar spicy scent of Rev washed over me. He dragged my head closer to him as we continued walking and smacked a kiss to my forehead. "Hey, little bit. How was your evening?"

"Well, it didn't have the happy ending I was hoping for, but the bourbon Kai got me made up for it."

Kai barked out a laugh from my other side. "If a mid level bourbon is better than a fuck then you aren't being fucked right."

I swear Rev actually growled at Kai, but I was throwing a frown Kai's way, so I couldn't be sure. I was about to say something when something else caught my attention, my hand gripping the fingers of Rev's hand where it's hanging over my shoulder. "What did you do to your hand? Are you okay?"

Rev just chuckled and turned his fingers to give mine a squeeze before letting go again. "I'm fine, little bit. Just accidently hit something hard. I'm all good."

Kai starts cackling beside me, and I frowned in his direction before looking back at Rev's grinning face. Focusing back on the walk to our apartment, I dismissed it; if they aren't concerned then I won't be either.

The memory fades away, instantly replaced by another. It's the way it was every night, like my mind wasn't satisfied with tormenting me with only one memory alone.

I heard stories that in hell, the thing that tortures the souls isn't the fires of hell themselves, it's the memories of our loved ones and our happy moments played on repeat. A reminder of the life we could no longer have and the people we could no longer touch.

If that were the case, then I lived in hell every single night.

The red was fading from my hair so I knew it was time to dye it again. I was toying with the idea of some shade of purple; Kai had just gotten a new tattoo on his neck with a swirl of purple at the heart of it. The color had been on my mind ever since.

I knew that Dead Devil's night was coming up soon so whatever color I chose, that seemed like my best day to do it.

We were all in the kitchen cleaning up after our weekly dinner and even though Rev wanted me to just sit on the couch and wait for them, I preferred helping and spending as much time with them as I could. "What do you think of the color purple?"

Kai looked at me in confusion, though he still had a grin on his face. "Why?"

I flicked a section of my hair that had fallen out of the loose bun I put it in earlier. "Time for a new color."

He laughed before putting on a fake pout. "Awww, but we liked the red, it helped advertise the too hot to handle attitude."

I gaped at him in indignation.

Rev flashed a grin. "Why not just go with a rainbow and then you wouldn't have to choose."

"Too much work," I responded with a scowl, still wanting to growl at Kai.

"Hell no, we don't want any of those dipshits deciding they want to 'chase the rainbow'."

This time, I do growl at Kai, flicking the cloth in my hand at the bare patch of skin above his sweatpants. He just grabbed the cloth and pulled me toward him to start tickling me. I wriggled in his soapy arms as he cackled hysterically at me.

Rev grabbed my chin, causing us to stop playing. "No matter what color you choose, you will always be beautiful to us." Stealing the cloth from my hands, he pulled me away from Kai and pushed me in the direction of the couch. "Now go pick a movie out, this is almost done."

Grumbling under my breath, I stomped across the room, and I swear I heard him call me a good girl under his breath. I just flipped him the bird and got laughter in response.

I can feel the tears leaving paths of sadness down my face as I start to wake. I wipe at my eyes desperately, as though simply dismissing the tears will push the memories back into their box in my mind. But my heart aches too much.

Rolling onto my side, I allow myself to sob into my pillow. It has been a year since that fateful night, and the pain in my heart is still a fresh and open wound. My body may have healed, but my heart and mind would always remind me that sometimes the worst part wasn't the physical pain at all.

RYLAN

C losing the bathroom cabinet in front of me, I take in my reflection.

I just finished dyeing my hair in honor of their memory, but seeing the fresh violet color makes my heart speed up and a wave of sadness wash over me.

Controlling my breathing and steeling my spine, I force myself to look at every part of my reflection in the mirror.

I have plans for the night. It is Dead Devil's night after all.

The plans I have, though, are vastly different from all the other years.

After I woke up in the care of an older police officer, David, who hid me away and nursed me back to health, I started making my plans.

When David told me that the twins were dead, it just fueled the burning rage that consumed me. He told me about coming across the scene at our home the following morning. He at first assumed that we were all dead, but then I made a noise.

He then quickly picked me up and got me to a doctor he knew to try to save my life.

He succeeded.

I then spent many weeks recovering in David's spare room while plotting my revenge. And then when I was back on my feet, I started to expand on those plans.

After what happened, I did consider myself lucky to have not had any lasting issues. The doctor that David had taken me to managed to get a massive amount of antibiotics into me as well as the morning after pill. I had scarring all over my chest and stomach, but it was easily covered with clothes.

David knew about my plans for the night, and had even gotten me as much information as he could to assist me. Including the identities of the men who attacked me.

But a few months ago, he was killed in a shootout at a local liquor store near his house.

From that moment, I was truly alone.

And I had nothing left to lose.

I stayed in David's house after he died. It was even further out of the city than the apartment I lived in with the twins. It was small, only a two bedroom little home, but it was all I needed.

Criminals and crime lords ruled the city. Power was in the hands of those who killed to take it and rule over everyone else below them. It was a cesspit of evil and corruption. An almost dystopian landscape of abandoned and ruined buildings. Most places in and around the city were not monitored or maintained. Law was minimal at most times, but there was none at all tonight. And I was going to use that to my advantage. Just like the men who attacked me and killed the twins did.

But I was going to give new meaning to the name Dead Devil's night. Because technically I was dead. Those men were going to meet the devil tonight, and I would be the one to introduce them.

I had spent the last two months following each of the men closely from the shadows. I now had their routines completely memorized. I knew their likes, their dislikes, every little detail about them.

At this point, I could probably predict when they needed to take a piss.

I lived and breathed them for months, perfecting my plans.

Taking another deep breath, I put a final touch on my light mascara and added a touch of gloss to my lilac painted lips. My reflection looked like a picture of innocence. My dark blue eyes are large and framed with black lashes, my skin pale and my cheeks rosy.

Paired with my newly refreshed violet hair, I appear sugary sweet.

But it was just that, an appearance. It was skin deep.

There was no innocence left in me. The plans I have are the opposite of innocent, but I need to look sweet as pie to get into some of the places I need to go. And to get the attention of who I need to.

Finishing in the bathroom, I make my way back to my bedroom. One of the walls is covered in photographs, plans and maps. But five images take center stage on that wall. The five men whose images are burned into my memories.

As I pull on my long black boots, I look at that wall. Refreshing myself again of all the details, even if I don't really need to.

The images are pinned to the wall, one above the other, and looking at each image, I let the memories play in my mind. I worked hard to move past the trauma of that night so that I could remember without breaking down. The last thing I need tonight is to have a trauma response while I get my revenge.

At the end of the column of images on the wall is Karver Walkin.

He was the first one in the door that night. He had instantly swung the bat in his hand at the closest target: Rev. I remember screaming as I watched the wood hit Rev's body, the spikes wrapped around the end tearing at his clothes and flesh as he tried to fight against Karver. But he was distracted by the next person through the door.

Damien Kane. The second image on the wall.

He went straight after Kai, who was on his way to help Rev. Damien also had a spike-wrapped bat. The bats that Rev and Kai had never stood a chance. The arm that Kai used to grip his weapon was shredded. Damien landed the spikes in Kai's upper arm and dragged them down to his elbow.

Next in the door and on the wall is Kasen Jekle.

By then Karver already had Rev on the ground, landing blow after blow. But Kasen took pleasure in tying up Rev's hands and feet.

Then came Ash Dean.

He also had rope in his hands that he used on Kai.

And while I screamed, they just laughed. Cheering each other on as they took turns using their weapons on the twins.

I was so busy concentrating on the twins that I missed the last person to enter the apartment.

Silas Holt.

But he didn't miss me.

The pain that exploded across my face and the impact of the strike sent me crashing to the floor. Silas was the one that dragged me across the floor of our home by my hair until I was in the center of what was our living room.

He was the one who ordered the other men to move the furniture out of the way and position Rev and Kai so they could see everything they did to me. He was the one in charge of them, moving everyone around like pawns in his own twisted game.

He was the one that gave the orders for them to stab the twins.

He was the one that gave the order to assault and stab me.

He was the last one to force himself inside me.

There were no reasons given for the attack.

They didn't care about our lives or who we were. From what I could tell, we were just entertainment for them.

They probably don't even remember me.

But they would soon know my name. And they would leave my life in the same order that they entered it.

And they would go to hell regretting ever meeting Rylan Coal.

RYLAN

The sun is just creeping low in the sky as I pull on my purple leather jacket.

I paired it with a flared black leather skirt and a low cut cream blouse that was just sheer enough to hint at the black bra I was wearing underneath.

Yes, I need to look innocent, but I also need to look sexy as well. And after doing some research, the leather would be easy to clean any blood off of. Practicality for the win.

But just in case, I had multiple changes of clothes in a bag that I threw into the trunk of David's car. It had taken me a little bit to start using it after David died, but in the end, I was thankful the twins had given me at least a few lessons so I could get around. Because tonight, I needed it.

I check the supplies in the trunk along with the bag for the final time. I would need to be careful that the vehicle didn't fall victim to the chaos of the night.

It isn't a flashy car; it was an older nondescript sedan in navy blue. It had no special accessories that called attention to it and the windows were clear so everyone could see that there was nothing inside to steal.

In other words, it was a 'nothing to see here' sort of car. The whole point of it is to blend in and last the night.

I already knew where Karver would be, they were all creatures of habit. And Karver's habit at this time of day was a fuck at his local whore house. Well I hoped they all stuck to their normal habits and routines tonight, otherwise shit was going to get real.

Sliding into the driver's seat, I check the time and realize that I need to hurry my ass up or I would be cutting it a little too close.

I make the quick drive to Ninth Street and pull up down the street from Karver's favorite spot. It's run down and seedy, but there is nothing surprising about that. The fact that it's still open for business on Dead Devil's night speaks volumes.

Stepping out of the car, I can already hear some of the screaming and chaos starting closer to the heart of the city. I couldn't see anything through the buildings yet, but the sound of glass shattering and laughter was faintly reaching me. I knew the closer I got to the center of the city, the more difficult it was going to get, and the harder it would be to hide.

Opening the trunk of the car, I slide two knives into my long boots, tucking them in sheaths so only enough of the handle shows that I can pull them out easily. I had already tested it and knew that when I pulled them out the sheaths would stay in the boots for convenience.

I had already done a lot of groundwork leading up to tonight. There were supplies positioned where I needed them, hidden from thieving hands. Or in some cases, even placed in plain sight weeks ago, so they didn't raise questions tonight.

But I still had plenty in the trunk of the car if something did happen outside of my control. I had spent too long planning this night that I was not going to let anything ruin it.

Reaching further in, I pull out a small case. Opening it, I grab the pretty steel ring I kept hidden there, sliding it onto my finger. It didn't look like anything much. But then again, neither did I.

Adding another couple of knives into the inside pockets of my jacket, I close the trunk of the car again, shoving the keys into one of the zippered parts of my jacket for safekeeping. I make my way across the street and towards my destination. The gravel and broken glass crunches under the soles of my boots.

If I have timed it right and he sticks to his schedule, Karver should be here shortly, and I need to be in the right place.

The closer I get to the whore house, the more I can hear what was going on inside the building. The exaggerated moans and porn worthy sounds from inside almost make me roll my eyes. I doubted any of the men inside even knew how to use their cocks properly enough to make it even slightly pleasurable for any of the girls.

Knowing Karver will be approaching from close to the back, I move around the side of the building and lean against the wall. Pulling out a packet of cigarettes and a lighter from another of my jacket pockets, I quickly light one up and tuck them back away. Nothing to see here, just a whore taking a smoke break from sucking cock.

Or at least that's the look I was aiming for.

I had done enough research to know that he had a type. If pretty, innocent looking slut was a type.

The cigarette was at least doing a good job of dulling the smell of piss and garbage that was coming from the alley behind the whorehouse. I knew from experience it was stronger back there.

I close my eyes briefly, taking in all the sounds for a moment. It was a symphony of disgust and depravity. But suddenly under that was the crunch of footsteps on gravel and glass.

Perfect. Show time.

Opening my eyes again, I flick the ash from the end of the cigarette in my hand and glance in the direction of the approaching figure. But not for long. I can't look too eager.

Even after looking at his photo every day and stalking him for months, just seeing him still makes me burn with hatred. His hair is buzzed close to his head and the blond color makes him look almost bald. He is covered in tattoos, there are even some on his face, and he is dressed in loose jeans and a wife beater.

Taking another drag, I cross an arm across my chest under my breasts, loosely holding my other elbow. It pushes my decent sized breasts further up in my blouse, making them more noticeable.

I tilt my head down as though I am looking at the ground in front of me before flicking another look in his direction from under my lashes. He's now a lot closer, and I can tell I have his complete attention. It was predictably easy.

His pace slows as he gets closer, coming to a stop only a few feet away. "Hey pretty little thing, you on a break?"

Bingo.

Time to see just how good my acting skills are.

I tilt my head back again, giving him a better view of my face as I watched him, but not a full view. This would be over before it begins if he remembers me.

"Can't work all the time, right?" I respond, taking another drag on the cigarette.

He chuckles in response. "You new? I haven't seen you before."

Good.

Looking up, I give him a little playful smile. "I'm new, just started. Not sure if I'm going to stay here, though. The cut they give us is pathetic."

Internally, I hope he isn't super loyal to whoever owns the fine establishment behind me.

A slow grin slides across his face as his eyes give me another once over. I feel like scrubbing myself clean just from having him look at me.

"How long is your break, pretty? I could give you all the cut I would have paid inside."

I let a flirty smile play across my lips as I flutter my eyes a little and pretend to think about it, tugging my lip between my teeth. His eyes focus straight on the movement, and I let go of my lip to give him a full look at them as I part them. I know he's fantasizing about my lips now, and I have to hold back a shudder at the thought.

"I'm sure I could stretch it depending on what you want. Like I said, not sure I'm staying here anyway, so it won't matter to me what they think."

His grin gets wider and more shark-like as he takes a few steps back in line with the alleyway and indicates to it with a jerk of his head. "Well then, pretty, let's negotiate for a little fun away from prying eyes." *Hook, Line and Sinker.*

I smile slyly and flick my cigarette away, following him as he walks backwards into the alley, as though he doesn't want to let me out of his sight. Oh, don't worry Karver, I'm going to be the last thing you ever see.

He keeps walking backward through the clear path that I previously made until his back is against a protruding brick wall toward the end of the alley. It's darker here, harder to see. Perfect.

I use a hand to push against his chest, flattening him more against the brickwork. I see a small flinch cross his face, and I let a look of concern cross my own. "Are you okay? Did I hurt you?"

He grins again, disregarding the moment in an effort to look like a macho man. "Of course not, sweetheart, pretty little thing like you couldn't hurt me."

I let the smile cross my lips again as I take a few steps away again, letting one of my hands slowly slide down the center of my blouse. "Do you like what you see? I do try to look extra pretty for my clients." I look down at my fingers as they play with the fabric a little, peeking up at him again through my lashes. "And you are a very giving client, right?"

His body is starting to relax into the moment as he watches my movements with a twisted grin. "Of course, I'll be extra giving for you, pretty girl."

I let my fingers walk further down my body until they reach the edge of my skirt, hooking one of the fingers on the material and ever so slightly dragging it up an inch. His eyes are following the movement with an eagerness that almost makes me nauseous. I stop and pretend to pout a little. "How giving though? I still don't see any money. Maybe I should just go back inside..."

Letting the material drop again, he frowns for a second in disappointment; the grin returning to his face quickly as he digs his wallet from his baggy pants. He opens it and drags out a wad of cash as he looks at me, probably hoping I will be impressed by it.

"I want to bury my dick inside you, but I also want to see those pretty lips wrapped around it too."

I give a fake giggle, but don't move. I just keep watching him. "Both is extra."

He chuckles and just folds up the wad of cash and holds it out to me. "I'm sure this will cover it and more. Something tells me you're worth it."

That does actually make me laugh, but I'm sure not for the reasons he thinks. "Oh, I absolutely am."

He frowns slightly, his eyes flicking down to the money in his hand. The frown deepens as his eyes come back up to mine and he takes a long blink.

I wait for another moment and when he doesn't move anymore; I let a real smile spread across my lips. I step closer to him again and put on a fake concerned look. "Are you okay? Are you sure this pretty little thing didn't hurt you?" I grin again. "Oh, that's right, you can't respond, right? Can't speak, can't move."

Moving forward, I pluck the money from his fingers and slip it into my pocket. I hate the man, but money wasn't something I would ever throw away. I don't bother counting it, not like I really care. Money isn't really the goal. I push his arms back down to his sides and tilt my head as I look into his eyes. "But you can feel." Holding my hand up in front of his eyes so he can see the tiny needle on the underside of the ring. "Tetrodotoxin. It's amazing what you can find on the black market when you're determined enough."

I remove the ring and throw it to the side. I have another one of them in the trunk of the car, and this one is useless now.

Reaching down, I pull out the knives from my boots. They are long and wicked sharp.

"Look, I'm sure whatever you thought was going to happen here would have been a ton of fun for you. But from what I remember, your dick was pretty pathetic." I grin as I hold up the knives for him to get a good look and for it to sink in, what is about to happen to him. "You may not remember me, but I remember you. We met a year ago. A year ago tonight, to be exact."

I see his eyes widen, and a garbled noise comes from him.

"Oh, you remember me now? I'm sure you are sorry, but it's just a little too late for that. You killed my best friends. Now let me see if I have the order correct. It was their arms you attacked first, right?"

With that, I stab the knives into the fleshy parts of both arms and drag downward. Blood starts gushing from the wounds as Karver makes a louder, garbled cry. His attempt at screaming, I'm sure. Either way, it's too much noise.

I pull the knives back out of his flesh and hold the bloody tips against his lips. "Hey now, none of that. I know I need to be quick, but please allow me to at least enjoy this for a moment without having to listen to you whine like a baby."

Stepping back, I look at him and the blood running down his arms. Some of it has already started to stain his white tank red.

"Now what next? Oh yes, there were stab wounds to the stomach." I plunge the blades into the flesh there, burying them deep and turning them as I pull them back out. He didn't listen to me and that awful noise is still coming from him, so I point the knives at his face again. "Stop it, you're annoying me. I'm trying to enjoy this, remember? Hush."

There are tears streaming from his eyes. And fuck, that feels good to see.

Taking a moment, I swing a couple of chains down from where I stored them a week ago. I wrap a chain tightly around one arm and bolt it in place on the wall, repeating the process with the other arm.

"You know what came next, right?" I slide the blades between the skin of his hips and the fabric of his jeans, jerking outwards in both directions. The knives cut through the fabric like butter. I'm not sure if I consider it lucky or unlucky that he wasn't wearing any underwear underneath when his jeans fell to his ankles. What little there is of his flaccid dick hangs between his legs. "You remember now, don't you? Raping me with that pathetic little dick. I suppose I should be glad you're a two pump chump."

I cross my arms over and slide the blades to either side of his shriveled flesh, pausing to look at his eyes again. "Did you even take the time to find out who it was you raped? Did you ever learn my name? Or the names of the men with me that you killed?"

His face is a mess of tears and snot and flecks of blood. I'm actually surprised he hasn't passed out yet, but I'm happy not to have had to waste an ammonia capsule on him.

"Their names were Rev and Kai Draven. My name is Rylan Coal. Remember that when you reach hell. And when they ask your name, make sure to tell them; it's Dead Devil Number One."

I move my arms in a quick motion; the blades acting like scissors in his flesh. After giving him a moment to scream to himself at the loss of his dick, I then slide the blades across his throat, silencing him for good. The noise was too annoying to wait any longer.

I was right, though. I was going to need that change of blouse.

It was surprising that there was still so much blood able to come from his neck, the warm liquid hitting me and dripping down my skin. I frown. I was going to need to account for that with the others.

Pulling a towel that I stored behind some garbage in the alley, I wipe down my jacket and skirt. I remove the jacket to pull off the blouse, and wipe my skin before putting the jacket back on over my black leather bra.

I really hope there is no blood on my face. I don't have time to reapply my makeup now.

Making sure I wiped off all visible blood from my body and blades, I throw the towel and blouse into a tin can positioned next to the body. Pulling out another cigarette and lighting it, I breathe a sigh, taking a long drag before throwing the lit cigarette into the can. The instant whoosh of it igniting the fuel soaked material in the bottom is satisfying, as was the little wave of heat that hit me.

Turning away and walking out of the alley, I make my way back toward the car. I have plans. I have a timeline to stick to.

One down, four more to go.

REV

I narrow my eyes at the sight in front of me. We had plans for Dead Devil's night. And someone is already ruining them.

We tried to time it right, knowing that the asshole Karver would be leaving the whorehouse at a certain time. Like he does every day.

He would be relaxed enough not to see us coming or put up as much of a fight.

But when he didn't appear I almost thought that, like last year, his routine was different. Then we noticed the fire behind the building.

I guess I can't be too upset, he looked like he died a bloody and painful death. We can only assume that he pissed off one too many people in the whorehouse and they took out the trash.

I cross my arms across my chest as I take in the carnage.

From the moment we woke up in that derelict hospital, we made plans to hunt down the men who invaded our home. The men who murdered the love of our lives.

Starting with Karver.

It seemed fitting that we did it on the anniversary of the day they took everything from us.

We both loved Ry since the moment she came into our lives, we just hadn't realized it until we were forced to move out of the foster home. Before then, we tried our best to fuck her out of our systems. But nothing worked, we always came back to the same thing, she was ours, she was meant for us.

She was the missing piece that connected our souls and made us one. One family, one love.

And they killed her.

Not just killed her, they utterly destroyed her. And for that, they had signed their own death warrants.

We weren't even sure what they did with her body. Taken for their own depravity, we assumed.

When those men entered the home we had created for her, our safe haven, all of our thoughts had been focused on protecting her. But we never predicted how many would storm our home, or the weapons and violence they used.

Even as the pain ripped through me and the spikes tore into my flesh, all I could focus on were her screams.

And then came the living nightmare they forced us to watch as we lay there dying from the knife wounds, our blood spreading across the floor of what had been our home. Our safe place.

The feeling of utter devastation I felt when I woke up alive and without her still haunted the back of my mind. And after lengthy discussions with Kai, I knew he felt the same.

Kai huffs out a breath beside me and allows the spike covered bat in his hand to smack against the ground. "Well, that was anticlimactic."

He steps forward and lifts the end of the bat to push Karver's head back and look at his face. Looking back at me, he grins. "Somehow I don't think he enjoyed Dead Devil's night as much this year."

My own grin pulls at my lips in response.

I narrow my eyes again as I look a little closer at the blood covered body from head to feet, noticing something I didn't the first time. "Is that what I think it is?"

Kai looks at where I'm indicating and then jumps back with a grimace, his hands automatically going toward his own junk. "Jesus, fuck. I wonder if he was still alive when that happened."

Even I flinch at that thought.

We missed the chance to take our revenge on Karver, but at least we knew he suffered anyway. "We should get out of here before anyone else comes along that might not be so happy about this prick's death."

Nodding in agreement, Kai gives the body one last look before turning with me and heading back out of the alley. Our motorcycles were parked further down the road closer to the city.

Once we reach them, we return our bats to the holders we created for them. The ones that matched the four others of the same kind around the front of our motorcycles.

The next one should be easier.

Damien Kane.

At this time of day he was usually at the pool hall only a few blocks closer to the city. Buying and doing drugs before he dragged his ugly ass further into the city to follow orders like a good little soldier.

Swinging a leg over my bike, I give Kai a renewed look of determination. "Let's keep moving, we have places to be."

Kai grins and swings his leg over his own bike. "And people to kill."

RYLAN

Parking the car a block away from the pool hall where my next target routinely frequented, I can hear the chaos even louder the moment I open the car door. I know a part of that is the noise of the pool hall itself, the laughter and screams echoing through the streets.

I put on a skin tight black tank underneath my jacket. It molds to my curves and after accessorizing with a few thin steel chains to my neck and rings to my hands, it gives the outfit a more grungy look. Perfect for the pool hall. Adding a couple more items to the outfit from the little case, I call it good enough.

Quickly checking my face in a small mirror, I make sure there is no obvious blood on my skin before locking it all up and starting toward my destination. It wouldn't really matter if there was blood there. I already checked the inside of the building a few times and the lighting was murky at best.

Damien only liked to play pool long enough to find his next fuck and score his next high. If I timed it correctly, then he should have a slight alcohol buzz already and be one game of pool in.

Pushing my way through the door and into the building, I'm met with a cloud of smoke and a blast of music and noise. There are barely clothed women everywhere, draped over guys that look like they have spent too much time high and drinking to be good at anything. Even now, in some corners of the large room filled with pool tables and people, I can see women bent over as creeps pump pathetically away at them.

It only takes moments for me to spot my target at one of the pool tables at the side of the room, still playing, but with a few girls in skimpy outfits trying to grab his attention. I've been here enough in the shadows to not instantly draw attention.

He has medium length brown hair. Just long enough to pull back into the knot behind his head and show off the undercut and the tattoos that cover the skin showing above his black shirt. The tattoos stretch across his skin, from his shirt across the back of his neck and even on the sides of his head. He may have been attractive at some point, but too many drugs and too much power had gotten to him. He was a piece of shit that would have been more fitting in the sewers below the rotting city, but even now the girls still tried to get his attention for the potential of being on his arm at the next city event in the hopes of catching a bigger fish.

Good luck girls, but I'm setting this river on fire.

After my initial scan of the room, I walk up to the bar, not paying close attention to anything in the room, but still aware of everything.

I know the moment I have his attention. It's akin to the feeling of skeletal fingers sliding along my skin. Cold and creepy as fuck.

Ordering a bourbon that I'm not going to actually drink, I see Damien indicate to the bartender from the corner of my eye. Right on schedule.

I knew he wouldn't be able to resist something new and shiny.

When the bartender returns with my drink and I go to give him the money for it, he waves me off. I raise an eyebrow at him, and he just indicates where Damien is standing.

Finally turning my attention in his direction, I see he's already focused on me, leaning against an empty pool table, cue in hand. A small smirk appears on his lips when he sees he has my attention.

If only he knew he has had my attention for a year now, he wouldn't look so cocky.

Pretending to take a sip of the brown liquid, I can smell that it's higher quality than what I ordered, but that still won't make me actually drink it. I knew that the bartender was on Damien's dime and regularly slipped things into the drinks of unsuspecting girls. But he was a problem for another day.

Slowly making my way over to where Damien is standing, I allow him to look his fill, seeing his eyes heat in appreciation. But not in recognition.

Trailing a finger along the edge of the table, I step closer and give him a coy smile. "Hi there."

He grins in response. I can almost see the thoughts running through his mind, thinking that it's his lucky day. He's about to have the unluckiest day of his life.

"Hey, sweet thing."

Even his voice sounds oily, dripping in fake honey tones.

I raise an eyebrow at him with another smile. "Sweet thing?"

He chuckles in response, and I force down a shudder, the memory of that sound from a year ago tugging at my mind. Stepping closer, he brushes a finger across my collarbone.

If I didn't need to play a part, I would have snapped that finger the moment it got close to me, but patience is a virtue. And I have a shit load of patience.

"Yeah, you look good enough to eat. What's a sweet thing like you doing here?"

I struggle not to roll my eyes at the pickup line.

Instead, I let my smile get wider as I keep thinking about the end goal and flutter my lashes at him. He continues to trail a finger along the edge of my tank and when his finger scrapes along the plastic bag tucked into my bra, I almost grin at just how easy this was turning out to be.

Because with Damien, I may be the hook, but what is tucked into my bra was definitely the line to drag him in. He rubs his finger across the plastic a little harder and the edge of it peeks out from where it's hidden.

"I don't like partying alone." I respond to him finally, giving him a sly smirk so now he will know exactly what I'm talking about.

He chuckles, and I feel his fingers pinch the edges of the bag, but I grab his hand before he can pull it out.

"I don't like crowds, though. Maybe we can have a private party." Sliding my other hand up his black shirt, I purposely let my nails scrape against his chest and hear his breath hitch.

And he takes the bait.

Grabbing my hand, he throws the cue in his hand onto the table and turns away to lead me behind him, toward the back of the building. I ignore all the hostile looks thrown my way by the other girls in the room while I silently follow behind him. I already knew where he was leading me. I had watched him take this path several times over the weeks of watching him from the shadows.

I let a true smile flit across my lips as I walk behind him. He is a dead man walking, he just doesn't know it yet. But he would very soon.

He pulls me into a dimly lit staff room at the back; I already know it has a small couch and a table but not much else. But I still don't move my eyes away from the man in front of me.

I reach back and close the door behind me, flicking the lock as he watches and gives me what I'm assuming is his version of fuck me eyes.

All it does is make me want to dig his eyes out with a rusty spoon.

Reaching into my left bra cup, I bring out the little bag of white powder and hold it out to him with a grin. When his eyes flick to it, I see the moment his eyes squint and the flair of temper that flashes onto his face.

"Not too much there for a good party, sweet thing," he says. "Maybe I should have seen if there was a better party out there."

I laugh in response before pulling another plastic bag from my right bra cup with a grin. I pull a straw from both bra cups and offer him the one in my left hand. He waves it off before starting to cut the powder.

Knowing he is watching me carefully, I wipe a shelf close by and start doing the same with the contents of the bag in my hand. Putting the straw in my hand to the first line, I inhale, turning back toward him when I'm done to watch him lean over and inhale his first line.

He grins at me when he's done and puts his straw down to lean back on the couch with his arms spread, allowing the hit to take effect.

"Come here, sweet thing. I want to watch those tits move as you bounce on my dick."

I laugh, and even to my own ears, it has an edge to it. I don't move toward him, and he tilts his head with a slight frown.

"Get that ass over here," he demands.

I only grin at him in response and watch as a drop of blood starts making a slow path from his nose.

"I had a different party in mind," I respond as my grin gets wider.

His frown deepens, and he gives a slight cough as he sits up straighter. He looks at the other line of drugs he cut and then looks at where I left my other line. Then he looks back at me in confusion.

Stupid, pathetic man.

"Oh, don't worry about me, it was just yours that was bad. Hell, mine wasn't even drugs." I reach a hand out and dip it into the powder from my line and bring it to my mouth, flicking my tongue out to lick it from my finger. "Mmm, powdered lactose. It's what they use in the movies."

He coughs again and this time blood sprays from his mouth across the table in front of him, the droplets stark red where they land on the white powder.

I can see the panic entering his eyes as he tries to speak, only to cough up more blood.

"Oh, don't worry, yours was definitely cocaine. Along with a few extra ingredients just to make it that extra spicy for you." I flutter my fingers at him with a grin.

I hear the rattling in his chest as he struggles to draw breath into lungs that are already being eaten away by chemicals.

His hands start to claw at his own chest as his pain-filled eyes plead with me for help.

I hum a tune as I move closer to him. It was one of the twin's favorites, totally fitting for the occasion. "You don't remember me. Your friend Karver didn't remember me until just before I slit his throat, either. We met a year ago. My name is Rylan Coal. And the men you killed that same night were Rev and Kai Draven, my best friends."

Moving even closer, I watch as the veins expand under his skin, hardening and turning black. He is still aware. I see the fear and re-alization in his eyes. I knew he was feeling every last second of his life slipping away, feeling as the chemicals ate away at his insides.

And I watched every last second of it with satisfaction.

Once his hands fell limply to the couch and his eyes remained open, vacant and unseeing, I knew I needed to move on. Looking down at myself, I see a few specks of blood on my skin but otherwise this method had no mess.

It was cleaner than the last time, but not as good as cutting off his dick.

Frowning slightly to myself as I grab a cloth from a shelf and wipe off the blood, I consider the differences. I preferred the personal touch. This one felt too impersonal.

I'll have to account for that with the rest.

Throwing the cloth aside, I exit the room and turn toward the back exit instead of going through the main room. I don't want to draw attention, and leaving so quickly will draw attention.

Two down, three more to go.

Chapter 6

KAI

W e don't spot our target anywhere in the room. We had circled the pool hall now for a few minutes and he wasn't there.

But he should have been.

I walk up to the bar. Bartenders always know where the big players are. And in his mind, Damien is a big player.

After a moment of watching the guy behind the bar actively avoid looking toward us, I hold up a twenty. It only takes him seconds to come in front of us after that, asking what he can get for us.

"Where is Damien Kane?" I ask him as he goes to take the money from my fingers. But I don't let the note go until he sneers at me.

"Why should I tell you that?"

I raise an eyebrow at him and give him a look as though he isn't worth the money or time. "Boss wants him and he isn't answering his phone."

The reaction is almost instant, the color leaching slightly from his face, and a tremor running through his hand, still gripping the money as though he has forgotten what he was doing. He has never seen us before, never seen Damien's boss either, only knew him by reputation, just enough to be scared of someone who could be here on his behalf.

With a loud gulp, he points toward the back of the room to a darkened hallway. "He went into the back room with a piece of ass."

I let the money go and watch as he scrambles away from us, as though the demons of hell are on his heels. The thought almost makes me laugh out loud. We are so much worse.

Motioning to Rev, I make my way toward where the bartender indicated, inwardly hoping we aren't about to walk in on him balls deep in some skank.

As we turn the corner into the hallway, a flash of violet catches my eye seconds before the back door closes behind the girl that stepped out of it. I stop in my tracks as memories of the last time I saw that color hit me. Memories of Ry are never far from my mind. In that moment it was almost like a slap in the face to see someone with the same color hair she died with.

Rev puts a hand on my shoulder and squeezes. "What is it?"

I frown as I keep staring at the now closed door. "Just something I thought I saw." I shake my head. It won't do us any good to be dragged down by the memories when the night was still so young, and we had a lot more to get done.

Rev grumbles and moves around me to the back room. My head jerks toward him when I hear him swear viciously, taking the step to look into the room also.

Damien Kane was already dead.

It didn't look nearly as violent as Karver, however it did look like it had been painful. But, dead was still dead. And frustratingly not by our hands.

A growl leaves Rev as he takes in the room. But I only need to see one thing for my brain to take a leap that has me running. There had been someone else in that room. Another line of drugs was on a shelf away from the one in front of Damien.

I throw the back door open and look around as I run toward the street. I can hear Rev behind me, hissing at me to stop while trying not to draw attention to us. I make it to the street, but still don't see anyone else around. It was like the person I saw walking out the door disappeared like a ghost.

Rev catches up to me and grabs my arm on a growl. "What the fuck?"

After giving the street another look, I turn to him. "I saw someone leave out the back door as we were getting there."

He tilts his head with a frown. "You think some other guy is hunting these guys too?"

I give him an intense look as my mind races. "It wasn't a guy. It was a girl."

He scoffs at me and looks at me as though I'm delusional. And frankly, I'm starting to feel he may be right with the thoughts going through my head. "She had violet hair."

The color drains from his face and he blinks at me in disbelief. I watch as he tries to process what I just said. He looks around the street in a rapid movement before looking back at me.

"Are you sure you weren't imagining it? Could it have been the lights?"

Maybe I am going crazy. There was a good chance after everything.

"No. But there is only one way to find out," I respond and start jogging toward where we left our motorcycles. Rev swings his leg over his own bike moments after I get onto mine. "Who would they be going after next?"

I gave him a look. "The same person we were going after next, Kasen Jekle."

Rylan

E verything was going exactly to plan. These men were so predictable it was pathetic.

But then, at the same time, I wonder why last year was different.
Why are these same men not causing the same chaos they did only
twelve months ago? Why are they not out raping and killing again?

Not that I was sad that they weren't. It made my night that much
easier that they were following their normal routines.

I don't exactly remember when they attacked us that night, and it
is slightly disturbing to think that even last year they may have gone
through the same routines and habits they did every night. Before they
chose death as a hobby.

Shrugging it off though, I continue to watch Kasen walking in my direction. He doesn't know he's walking in my direction, he's just following the same path he does every night at this time.

It took me several weeks to pick this exact spot. I knew that I could get him when he reached his run down apartment just above me. But when I saw the path that Kasen walked to his apartment, I knew exactly how I wanted to do this. The memory of this man laughing as he kicked and stomped at Rev and Kai still haunts me.

So what I planned seemed fitting. Almost poetic.

Kasen let his dirty blond hair grow over the last year, past the point of being tidy, becoming more shaggy. He was lean and only slightly muscular. He looked like a surfer boy lost in a dark city while wearing black pants and a simple blue shirt. His hand was currently wrapped around an unopened bottle of bourbon. He picked one up every night on his way to his apartment.

He reaches the steps leading down from the street to the back entrance of his building. It is a stroke of luck that the back entrance is lower than street level. I watch with keen interest as his foot goes straight through the fake step that I created. The loud mechanical snap echoes through the small area.

Then comes Kasen's scream, like music to my ears.

If there is one thing I am truly thankful for tonight, it is that everyone ignores the sounds of screaming to stay safe in their own beds. I wasn't so thankful for that last year though.

I move from the shadows towards Kasen who doesn't even notice me. His entire focus is on his mangled leg and the bear trap that snapped shut on it.

It hadn't been an easy find, but fuck, it had been worth it.

For someone who was in what I imagined was some extreme pain, he still hadn't let go of the bottle of alcohol in his hand.

Forcing the smile off my lips, I look at the man in front of me clutching at the metal claws embedded in his leg. "Oh my god, are you okay?"

He looks up at me from where he is bent over his own leg, tears coating his face. It's such a pretty, pretty sight, it's hard not to smile at that alone.

"Please help me."

I tilt my head and start walking backward. "Please help me? Now why does that sound so familiar?" I stop walking at the end of the little alleyway and pick up the ends of two ropes that are on the ground. Exactly where I put them. "Oh, that's right, I remember screaming that same thing this time last year. And you just laughed."

I heave on the ropes in my hands as his eyes widen. The ropes were tied to two anchors sitting high on ledges. Those anchors had chains that wrapped around security bars that residents of the apartments on either side used to keep themselves safe from men like Kasen. And the ends of those chains were bolted to the sides of the bear trap embedded in Kasen's leg.

The anchors weren't as hard to come by as the bear trap was. In a derelict city, there were a lot of dilapidated boats in the little harbor.

As soon as the anchors slid off their ledges, it was like magic. And once again, the scream that leaves Kasen's mouth as the chains pull him into the air by his mangled leg was like music to my ears.

This time, he lets go of the bottle. I am happy that he did so while he was still mostly on the ground, so it just rolled along the concrete but stayed intact. Because when he finished being pulled by the anchors, he was dangling in the air by the bear trap, so far above the ground that I didn't even need to bend far to look into his face. The chains spun him so that he is now facing the mouth of the alley, on display for anyone walking.

I let him swing on the chains for a moment while I walk past him and pick up the bottle, taking a look at the quality of bourbon he buys. "Nice!" Setting it aside, I move back over to the crying and whimpering man.

Leaning down slightly, I look into his face. "Do you remember me now, Kasen?" I ask him.

He reaches out, trying to use his now free hands to grab onto me, but I'm just out of reach. "You can't be here. We killed you."

I do laugh at that, a grin stretching across my face. "Then I must be the ghost of Dead Devil's nights past, right?" He whimpers again. I reach down to pull the knives from my boots. "I know Karver and Damien didn't find out my name, but did you?"

The look on his face tells me everything I need to know. I was insignificant to him. Just another person to torture and kill among the many that he has probably killed.

"It's Rylan Coal. And those men with me were Rev and Kai Draven. They were the best people in this shitty world, and you killed them. Something tells me you won't forget those names now for the rest of your life."

I step forward and stab my knives into the flesh of his stomach before stepping back and out of his reach again. "Well, the few minutes you have left of your life, anyway."

There he goes, singing that sweet music for me again.

He's trying to put his hands against the stab wounds, but he is already so weak he can't raise his arms more than a few inches before they drop back down. Stepping back up to him I swing the knives high and then down, and his screams become more high pitched as the blades embed into his pathetic dick.

Then the music stops.

I pull the knives out and step back. I see he has lost consciousness.

I'm just contemplating using an ammonia capsule to wake him up when a strangled noise comes from behind me. Disappointment floods me, knowing that not only is my fun about to be cut short, but that I may need to take care of witnesses.

Turning slowly, I look into green eyes I never thought I would ever see again. I wonder if I am somehow a ghost after all. Because the two men in front of me surely are.

They can't be real. Maybe I have truly gone over the edge of insanity. All I can do is stare slack-jawed at them as they stumble closer to me with looks of shock that I'm sure mirror my own.

"Ry?"

I'm not sure which of them asks, but then we are all moving, colliding in a tangle of limbs.

"I thought you were dead."

"How are you here?"

"Where have you been?"

We are talking over each other. I can't stop my hands from moving across their skin, not believing that they are really here, in front of me. Their touch is familiar but foreign. Their hands are also touching me all over, their eyes searching over my whole body and taking in everything.

The swinging man behind me is now completely forgotten as I try to understand what I am seeing.

Rev wraps his big hands around the sides of my neck, resting his forehead against mine and looking deep into my eyes. "Little bit." His old nickname for me makes my heart clench and tears finally come to my eyes. "They told us we were the only survivors pulled from that building. How are you alive? Where were you?"

Bringing trembling fingers to his cheeks, I still can't believe my eyes as I touch the smooth skin there. "A cop pulled me out and hid me away to recover. He said you were dead. I thought you were dead, Rev. I've spent the last year planning to avenge your murders."

He lets a sardonic laugh slip out as he gives a slight shake to his head. "And we have been doing the same."

And then his lips are on mine and nothing else matters.

Chapter 8

RYLAN

I still think there is a fair chance I've finally cracked or this is a dream, but fuck if it isn't the best dream ever.

Rev's lips move over mine before his tongue flicks at the seam of my mouth, and I open for him instantly. His tongue plunges into my mouth to tangle with mine as he takes what he wants. His fingers press hard into the skin of my neck, pulling me closer to him like he wants to crawl inside of me completely.

My hands are clutching at him in response, trying to drag him closer to me and merge our bodies into one. He tastes like the grape gum he always used to chew, and to me that tastes like home and happy memories.

I feel his heart racing through the shirt he wears under his black leather jacket.

He moves back from my mouth, his breath panting softly across my lips as he looks deep into my eyes. But then I am turned in Rev's arms and Kai's mouth is devouring mine.

Kai pushes my back more solidly against Rev's chest as he presses himself to me, his lips and tongue moving against mine. The taste of caramel and coffee hits my senses and brings back moments of fighting with him over the caramel coffee syrup that Rev bought us.

I can't stop the moan when Rev's lips softly touch the back of my neck, leaving soft kisses in a path up to my ear as Kai continues to kiss me.

"The thing we regretted the most when we thought you were dead was not showing you how we really felt about you." Rev's voice is soft and full of emotion.

Kai finally allows me to breathe, resting his forehead against mine in a mirror of what Rev had done. "We love you, Ry. The only thing that kept us from following you in death was the thought of vengeance."

I don't even realize I'm crying until Kai pulls back and wipes the tears from my cheeks. "Vengeance has been all I have thought about for the last year. I couldn't let myself stop, or I would have broken. You were both my whole world. I'm sorry I didn't tell you," I whisper, closing my eyes as I try to pull myself back together.

Rev brushes my hair to the side and kisses my temple. "No one will ever take you away from us again. We will slaughter anyone that even tries."

A whimper and cry reminds me of the slaughtering I was in the middle of before they appeared.

Kai looks behind him at Kasen hanging from the chains, then he laughs. "Speaking of..." He grins as he looks back at me, the humor still dancing in his green eyes. "Can we join in on the fun?"

I chuckle in response, picking up my knives from where I dropped them in order to touch them. Just looking at them has the biggest smile on my lips. "Not sure there is much fun left in this one, but sure."

He steps back up to me, grabbing my neck and smashing his lips against mine in a quick, brutal kiss. "Fuck, you're beautiful."

Releasing me, he holds a hand out toward Rev, who passes a bat to him. A spike-wrapped bat like these men attacked us with. A giggle bubbles up and out of my lips as I raise an eyebrow at Rev with a pointed look at the bat in his hands.

Rev grins and swings the bat in a circle. "Fucking karma."

I cackle as he moves around me to stand next to Kai, who stands pushing the end of his bat against one of Kasen's stomach wounds. "You awake asshole?"

Kasen whimpers again in response.

"Good." I hear the humor in Rev's voice as he growls out the word. And then he takes the first swing.

It was like watching them play a gruesome game of pinata, taking turns to swing their bats at Kasen until they were covered in a red haze.

And fuck me, it was the first time in over a year that something has turned me on. Watching as they destroy one of the men who tried to destroy us has me all sorts of fucked up. I feel the beating pulse of my pussy as I watch their muscles bunch and move and the blood fly from their bats.

Maybe I cracked after all, because that shit is the hottest thing I have ever watched.

They stop after a few minutes and it's easy to see that Kasen is no longer with us. But I couldn't care less.

Both of them turn back towards me, panting. I'm not sure what is showing on my face, but after a moment I can see the heat burning like fire in their own eyes.

Kai is the first to reach me like a blood covered freight train. He picks me up and takes me along with him until my back is against the closest brick wall and his mouth is on mine again.

I moan loudly into the kiss as I wrap my legs around his hips, my hands fisting in his short hair. I don't care that I'm being covered in blood as Kai's body rubs against mine.

"Fuck," Rev curses from next to us as Kai's mouth moves from my lips to my jaw. Rev's bloody hand wraps around the front of my throat and he uses his fingers to turn my head toward him, forcing Kai's lips to the side of my jaw, his tongue licking up to my ear.

"Eyes on me, Ry." Rev says and I force myself to look into his green eyes. "If you don't want this, say so. If you need us to stop, we will."

I moan again as Kai's teeth gently tug on my earlobe. "Fuck me, please, I need to feel you."

Rev's fingers dig in harder in response, as though his restraint is being tested, but a pained look enters his eyes. "I don't want to make you remember them."

Reaching out, I take a handful of Rev's hair, dragging him closer to me. "Then give me new memories."

He doesn't hesitate again, his lips crashing into mine and his tongue plunging into my mouth to tangle with mine as Kai slowly lowers my feet back to the ground. I almost protest, not knowing what he is doing until his hands slide under my skirt, gripping the underwear I have on and tearing them from my body.

Then he has one of my legs over his shoulder and his mouth on my pussy, and I must officially be in heaven.

There is no other explanation, because the feel of his mouth on me is divine. Rev's mouth continues to devour mine as Kai licks from my opening to my clit, swirling his tongue around it before sucking it into his mouth.

The sound I make is obscene, but Rev swallows it, one of his hands moving to fist my violet hair. His other hand travels down into my bra and rolls my hard nipple between his fingers.

Kai's mouth continues to move, his tongue flicking, his teeth nipping at the sensitive flesh. I feel an orgasm slowly building. I haven't touched myself in over a year, too afraid of triggering my memories, but nothing about the way they touch me reminds me of that night.

Kai sucks my clit into his mouth again, at the same time he slowly pushes a finger into my pussy, and I tighten around him as he pushes me closer to the edge of oblivion. His tongue flicks as he adds another finger, thrusting them inside of me before curling them and scraping his teeth against me.

I lose it, screaming into Rev's mouth as I cum hard. My pussy pulses around Kai's fingers as he continues to suck and lick at me.

Rev moves his face back from mine and holds my head so that all I can see is him. "Give me another, Ry. I want to watch you cum on my brother's tongue."

Fuck, why is that so hot?

Kai pushes a third finger inside of me, and I know that Rev won't have long to wait. My body is already starting to tighten around Kai's fingers again. I'm already panting and moaning in response, my eyes staring into Rev's as I hurtle toward the edge again.

Rev leans closer and flicks his tongue against my panting lips before he nips at my chin. Kai's fingers are moving harder, thrusting into my pussy and curling to rub against that spot inside of me that I know is about to have me seeing stars.

"Cum for us, Ry," Rev breathes and I shatter, my scream echoing around the alleyway.

I'm coming back down from my orgasm when Kai moves my leg from his shoulder and slowly stands back up. Then he watches me with burning eyes as he sucks his wet fingers into his mouth, licking them clean like he is licking his favorite ice cream. And I have seen him lick an ice cream. The sound he makes is not something he makes when he eats ice cream, but it has my body throbbing.

Rev nips at me again. "Do you still want our cocks, baby girl?"

I moan, "Yes, fuck yes."

He doesn't ask again, moving in front of me and then lifting me up against the wall again. Kissing me deeply, he wraps my legs around him, and then I feel him undoing his pants. The first touch of the head of his cock against me has me moaning and dropping my head back against the bricks, my eyes fluttering closed as he bites and licks along my jaw.

And then he starts slowly pushing inside of me.

He is bigger than anyone that I've ever been with before. I can feel him everywhere, as he starts stretching me inch by inch.

The men who raped me have nothing on this man. There is no comparison, and yet panic starts to claw at my chest.

A whimper rips from me as a flash of memories from the previous year hits me.

Chapter 9

RYLAN

R ev stills, his hand coming up to grip my jaw. "Eyes on me," he growls, and I automatically obey. His green eyes lock with mine as he watches me focus back on him.

The panic eases, and my breathing slows down again.

Once he sees that I have calmed down, his fingers dig harder into my jaw. "Keep your eyes on me, baby girl. Don't look away, don't close your eyes, just watch me as I fuck you and make you ours."

Fuck if that doesn't have me dripping for him again.

He pulls his cock back until I almost lose him, but then he pushes back inside of me. My eyes don't leave his. I watch every emotion that crosses his face as he pulls back and then presses into me again.

When he's buried inside of me completely, he grinds his pelvis against my clit and my pussy tightens around him as I moan at the sensation. Pleasure crosses his face as he groans, then sets a steady pace, thrusting inside of me as he keeps his eyes locked with mine.

Then a stream of filth starts pouring from his hot mouth. "Your pussy was made for me, Ry. Such a perfect fucking pussy. That's it, baby girl, squeeze my cock with that perfect pussy."

I'm on the edge of cumming when he pauses and I growl. A grin flashes across his face and then he adjusts his arms. I catch sight of Kai behind Rev, his cock in his hand as he strokes and squeezes it, his eyes burning as he watches his brother fuck me.

Rev lets go of my jaw to hook my knees over his arms and grip my hips tightly. When he moves again, he is no longer gentle, and he doesn't hold back.

His hips snap forward, his skin slapping against mine as he thrusts his cock deep inside me.

I don't even recognise the sound that escapes me. "Fuck, yesss."

He chuckles, but starts moving faster and harder, setting a rhythm that has me moaning like one of those bitches in the whorehouse. And all the time his eyes don't leave mine and his mouth doesn't stop with the dirty filth. "You like my cock buried in this pussy, Ry? I wish I had done this years ago. You're ours, baby girl. Who does this pussy belong to?"

I moan in response, but he somehow wants me to think and respond to him. He slaps the skin of my hip hard and I clench around him. I'm so fucking close.

"Say it," he growls, his pace still not slowing.

"Yours," I moan in response.

"Good, now cum on my cock."

My body obeys him, like it too knows exactly who it belongs to. My orgasm hits me and nothing else matters but the rush of absolute pleasure sweeping me up like a wave.

My vision blacks out for the briefest moment but no memories come to me, it's just ecstasy and him. But when I blink again, he's all I can see.

His own pace stutters as my pussy tightens hard around him and with a low groan he follows me over the edge. It's the sexiest fucking noise I have ever heard and it's now become my new favorite soundtrack.

And the look on his face when I focus on it is what I assume mine looked like. Like he found heaven.

It's a look I want to see on his face every chance I can get. And if Kai gets that same look then even fucking better.

Rev leans in to me to brush his lips against mine before gently lowering my legs to the ground again. I chuckle because there is a good chance I'm not going to be able to stand for a little while. He just grins at me like he can read my thoughts and holds me against the wall while shooting a look over his shoulder at Kai.

Rev slides away from me only to have his body replaced by Kai, with a hand on my hip and one brushing some sweaty strands of hair from my face. His grin is big as he looks at my flushed face. "You all weak in the knees for us, gorgeous girl?"

I laugh as I drag his lips to mine. For twins, they kiss so differently. Rev is pure possession while Kai has a playful edge as his tongue flicks into my mouth, playing with mine until he deepens the kiss to scorching.

While he kisses me, my legs become steadier, so I take charge of the moment. Using my body pressed to his blood covered chest, I reverse our positions until his back is against the brick wall. Wiping my hand

and reaching down, I wrap my hand around his hard cock and savor the groans that come from him as I move my hand along his length.

When our lips part, his head falls back against the bricks and he looks at me with hooded eyes. "What are you doing, gorgeous?"

I grin at him and then lower myself to my knees. The ground is rough and hard against my skin, but I don't care. There is blood everywhere, all over us, all over the ground. It's dark and dirty, and I love it.

"Fuck," he groans as my tongue comes out to flick against the head of his cock.

"You got to taste me. Now I want to taste you," I reply, giving him another lick.

He growls softly and threads a hand into my hair, gripping it hard as he tilts my head back to look at him. "Don't tease, Ry. I've dreamed about watching those big blue eyes as you swallow my cock a hundred times."

My grin spreads even wider before I wrap my lips around the head of his cock and move slowly down his length. His hand tightens almost painfully, and he moans long and low. Looking back up at him from under my lashes, I see his focus is completely on me. His mouth is open slightly as he breathes heavily.

He is just as big as his brother, so I only make it halfway down his length, wrapping my hand tightly around the base of him that doesn't fit in my mouth.

"Fuck, you look so fucking good with those pretty lips wrapped around my cock."

I set a slow pace, moving my head up and down his hard length. I swirl my tongue around the head before taking as much of him as I can, my tongue continuing to flick and my teeth gently scraping against him. It's his turn to moan obscenely.

When I hum around him with my mouth as far as it will go, his hips jerk away from the wall, thrusting into my mouth and hitting the back of my throat. It makes me moan and hum around him harder.

His hand tightens even further and his other hand comes up to take another handful of my hair as I move back to just the tip. "I'm not sure how much longer I can control myself, Ry."

I lick the end again and grin. "Then don't."

He pulls my head away from him to lean down and brush his lips against mine. "You want me to fuck that pretty throat, gorgeous?"

"Yesss," I moan, loving the hold he has on my hair.

He growls again. "Relax your throat, and tap my hip if you need me to stop."

The first thrust of his cock back into my mouth has me gagging, but then he gives me a moment to do what he said and I force my throat to relax. His next thrust has him sliding a little into my throat. The next thrust he goes even further, his hands clenching in my hair and tilting it just the way he wants.

Then he is sliding in until my nose brushes the skin of his pelvis.

I moan and swallow around him and his control snaps. Holding my head, he sets a hard and vicious rhythm, fucking my throat the way he wants. And fuck if I'm not dripping and throbbing again from it.

Reaching down, I slide my fingers over myself, but Rev has already seen my intentions. He crouches down beside us, knocking my hand away and replacing it with his own. "From now on, you only cum on our fingers or cocks, baby girl."

He thrusts three fingers deep inside me, pressing the heel of his palm against my clit.

I'm moaning loudly around Kai's cock, my hands grabbing his blood soaked pants in some attempt to drag him closer to me.

"Yes, fuck, that's it. Swallow my cock. You're such a good fucking girl."

Rev's other hand comes up and wraps around my throat, squeezing gently as he thrusts his fingers inside me and grinds against my clit. It takes only seconds before I'm screaming my release around Kai's cock.

Two more thrusts and Kai is cumming deep in my throat as I struggle to swallow around him while coming down from my own climax. I give him one last lick as he pulls himself from my mouth, and he gives me a heated look in response.

Grinning, I stand back up and look around the alleyway again before walking over and picking up the bottle of bourbon. Unscrewing the lid, I take a deep swallow of the harsh liquor and then hand the bottle over to Rev.

I wander over and retrieve a towel I had stored behind some trash cans, using it to wipe as much of the blood from my body and clothes as I can. The tank is ruined, so I pull it off and throw it into the trash can closest to me.

Turning back to the guys as I shrug the leather jacket back on, I see their eyes heat at all the skin I have on display until they see the scars. The fury that crosses both of their faces heats my blood as I walk back toward them with two more towels.

They clean their own skin, loosing their shirts to the trash and putting their jackets back over tattooed and scarred chests. I could melt into a puddle at the sight of them. But the same anger burns in me when I see their own scars.

Setting the trash on fire I start walking backward out of the alley, grinning at them.

"Come on boys, we still have people to kill."

Chapter 10

REV

I can't believe she is alive.

Our girl is right in front of us with a grin lighting up her beautiful face. There is evil in her eyes and fuck, it's a good look for her.

When Kai mentioned that the girl he saw leave the pool hall had violet hair, I almost stopped breathing. But then I pushed away my hope that she was somehow alive. It had been a year, not only did she not come back to us, but why would she still have that hair color when she had only just dyed it that day last year?

But finding out she too thought we were dead, and that she was avenging us, just made it all that more clear. She owned us, body and soul, just the same way she is ours.

I would watch the whole city burn before I lost her again.

Looking across to where Kai is watching her, I see that slight crazy edge to his eyes that he's had for the last year. I know he feels the same way as me.

I don't think that there would even be anyone left alive when he pours gasoline on the flames if something happened to her again. He would pile the bodies high and light those fuckers on fire.

But I would be right there beside him.

They signed their own death warrants the moment they touched the Draven family.

Rylan

A sh Dean wasn't where he was meant to be.

I knew the risks of my plans when we had our fun after killing Kasen. But I knew Ash's schedule and routines back to front, so I wasn't too concerned at the time.

But that fucker wasn't where he normally was right now, and I didn't know where the little cockroach crawled to.

After we left the alleyway, the twins followed me on their hot ass motorcycles to Ash's apartment building on Third Street. But when we got there, it was empty.

I had changed into a new black mesh top over my bra and the twins keep sending me heated looks as though they both hadn't cum inside me not long ago. Admittedly, the moment I saw them on their motorcycles, I wanted to ride them on their bikes. But I had plans and this current situation was what happened when I allowed distractions.

Picking up one of the empty beer bottles on Ash's coffee table amongst the other trash, I throw it at the wall in frustration. Kai just grins at me and raises an eyebrow in response.

Huffing, I fist my hands on my hips. "Where the fuck is he?"

I see Rev tilt his head out of the corner of my eye and when I look in his direction, I notice he is looking at something in the other direction. He wanders across the room in the direction he is looking and moves some trash off the kitchen counter. Then he presses a button on the machine that's revealed.

"Ahhh man, are you there? Karver's dead man. Slaughtered. Ash, are you there?"

"Yeah, I'm here, what the fuck do you mean he's dead?"

"He didn't show up to the dropoff, so I went to the whorehouse, thinking he got distracted like last time. Man it was fucked up. He was strung up behind it, hacked up. They even cut his dick off."

Rev sends a vicious grin in my direction, and I can't stop my own grin in response.

"Fuck. Get Damien over there, he's closer."

"He's not answering either, man."

Kai chuckles, and I swear I hear him mumble under his breath something that sounded like 'Try a ouija board.'.

"For fuck sake, you're all a bunch of incompetent fuckers. I can't call Si with this shit, he's at the club. I'll be there shortly."

The recording cuts off with a bang as though Ash slammed the phone down. Rev laughs as he moves some more papers aside to unearth the old phone on the bench. "Not that we aren't grateful for making shit easy for us, but who the fuck still uses landline phones anymore?"

Kai shrugs. "Emergency line maybe?"

Rev picks up a beer bottle on the bench beside the phone. It's only half filled. "He didn't leave that long ago, this is still cold."

I frown, my thoughts moving rapidly through my mind. "We can't let him have the opportunity to warn Silas. We need to go back to the whorehouse and cut him off."

The look on Kai's face is far too eager, like a psychotic puppy. "Cut him off or cut him up? Does this mean we get to watch you play with knives again? Cause that shit made me hard as fuck."

I'm laughing as I walk out of Ash's apartment. I hear them following me as I make my way back down to the street, not bothering to sneak out the same way we snuck in. It's not like we were trying to creep up on anyone now.

Seconds from stepping out the front door of the building, I freeze, Rev almost running into my back with how suddenly I stop walking. What I see outside has a smile stretching across my lips. "Change of plans, boys."

Rev frowns before following my eyeline. "It can't be that easy."

Across the road and down a few buildings, crouched down beside his car changing the tire, is Ash Dean.

A hand takes hold of mine, spinning me back and into Kai's arms who then spins me around before bowing me backward like we are dancing. It was something we used to do all the time and laughter bubbles up and out of me. For the first time I see the real emotion in his eyes as he looks down at me.

"So how are we doing this, gorgeous? Somehow I think he might be on the defensive if he sees us coming," he asks as he returns me to an upright position.

"Then let's make sure he doesn't see you coming," I reply, putting my hand against the door.

Rev grabs my arm, stopping me and I almost growl in frustration. "Just give me a few minutes and trust me."

He uses a finger on my chin to tilt my face back toward him before brushing his lips against mine. "We do, just be careful."

With that he lets me go, and I push through the door, letting it swing closed behind me as I start moving along the sidewalk. Reaching inside my jacket, I retrieve what is stored there and put it on. I'm now in line with where Ash is finishing with putting the new tire on his car.

I look him over as I cross the street, pushing the rage back down. It wouldn't work to have that emotion on my face.

His brunette hair is short at the sides and long on top like the twins'. He doesn't have any visible tattoos, but likes to show off his status with gaudy chains. The type you look at and just want to choke him out with. He spends too long at the gym, and I know if it came down to a fair fight he would overpower me in moments.

Reaching out, I grab his shoulder and he jerks away from me sharply. "Oh, I'm so sorry, I was just trying to see if you needed any help." I flutter my lashes at him and try to look as innocent as I can.

Ash scoffs, brushing off his initial surprise as I knew he would the moment he saw I was a woman. "I got it, sugar, don't you worry your pretty head about it."

I stand to the side and clasp my hands behind my back, the picture of sweet and naive as he finishes with his tire and then stands up. He pulls a rag from his trunk after throwing his tools back in there and cleans the dirt from his hands.

"Are you sure I can't help with anything?"

He leans against the car and gives my body a slow look over. When his eyes reach my face he frowns slightly. For a moment I think he recognizes me, but he then dismisses it and gives me a condescending smile.

"Nah I have somewhere I need to be. But a sweet, innocent little thing like you shouldn't be out on a night like tonight."

I can't stop the laughter that escapes me. "I stopped being those things a year ago."

He frowns at me again, his eyes flicking over my face as he lets his hands drop to his sides. He scoffs at me again, but I can see the mental struggle starting to take place behind his eyes. "And what could you even do?"

The smile stretching across my lips gets even bigger; I just loved how men underestimate women. It made moments like this all the sweeter. "Maybe you should ask Karver what I can do. Or Damien. Or Kasen." He blinks at me owlishly. "I mean, you can't right this moment, but maybe when you get to hell you might want to broach that subject. Just out of curiosity."

I step closer to him again, he doesn't move away, and only the slightest flinch crosses his face. Because that's all the toxin will allow at this point.

Grinning, I look past him and back to the building I just came from and wave an arm. It only takes a moment before the twins are jogging across the street to meet me. Rev's hand fists a handful of my hair and drags my lips to his while Kai pokes a finger at Ash's cheek.

"That's fucking creepy." Kai shudders and turns to me, dragging me from his brother's arms. "Hey, gorgeous."

Kai gives me a hard smacking kiss as Rev circles Ash's still body until he returns to stand beside me again, flicking a hand at Ash. "So how did you do that?"

I pull the ring off my finger and show them the sharp needle in the underside. "Tetrodotoxin, it's what I used for Karver too. He can see and feel everything, but he can't talk or move."

Kai cackles beside me. "Savage. I fucking love it. So Karver actually felt it when you sliced and diced his dick?"

Nodding, I grin at them. I don't care that my crazy is showing.

Rev once again fists my hair and pulls my mouth to his, kissing me deeply before pulling back and mumbling against my sensitive lips. "So fucking perfect for us." He lets go again and smiles at whatever he sees on my face. "So what is your evil mastermind plan for this asshole?"

Looking back at Ash, I watch his eyes as I say what's in my mind. "Did you know that a burning car can get as hot as fifteen hundred degrees Fahrenheit?"

The look of panic and fear that fills Ash's eyes is priceless, and the shocked laughter from the twins is even better.

"Besides, it's Dead Devil's Night. Burning cars are common tonight, and no one gets near them until the cleanup in the morning."

"Fucking perfect," Kai gasps out between his laughter.

Once the twins control their laughter, we move Ash until he is sitting in the driver's seat of his car. When I start opening the windows a fraction, they look at me in confusion.

"The fire won't spread without oxygen, boys. We want a furnace, not an oven."

Rev chuckles but starts doing the same on the other side of the car. I open the cap on the car's gas tank and then once the twins have stepped away, I reach under the car and yank the fuel line away from the tank and move back. The street thankfully has a small slope to it so that when the fuel starts spreading from under the car, it creates a small stream in our direction.

Reaching into the pocket of my jacket, I pull out the packet of cigarettes and offer them to the twins. They were the ones that got me into the habit in the first place. They each take one with a chuckle while I light two in my mouth at once.

Taking one from my mouth I flick it at the spreading gas and watch with glee as it ignites, then I take a drag from the other as we watch the flames race back toward the car.

I do strangely wish that Ash wasn't paralyzed because the sound of his screams would have been so beautiful, but instead all we got was the muffled cries that to me just sounded annoying.

Taking drags of our cigarettes, we stay there and watch the fire eat away at the car and then at Ash. Before long, the annoying sounds he was making stop and the car is completely engulfed.

We all turn away and they both wrap an arm around me as we head back toward my car and the bikes.

"Four down, only one more to go."

Chapter 12

RYLAN

We just reached my car when I found my back pressed hard against it and Kai's lips were moving hungrily against mine. He presses himself against me while gripping my hips, grinding against me and turning me on even more than I already am.

He slows the kiss to a stop, almost reluctantly pulling back from me a fraction, his lips still brushing mine as he speaks. "That was so hot, I really want to fuck you over the hood of this car until you're screaming my name for the whole goddamn city to hear who you belong to."

I hum because fuck yes. "Then why don't you?"

"Because we don't have time on our murder schedule to add more bodies if they see your gorgeous ass."

I grin wickedly at him before pushing him away. He looks confused for the two seconds it takes for me to unlock the car and jerk open the back door. When I sit down on the back seat and scoot further into the car, his eyes are almost as hot as the car fire we just left behind.

He licks across his lower lip as he steps up to the open car door. "Hands and knees, beautiful. We only want your mind on us when we fuck you."

Understanding and appreciation hit me briefly, but the moment I turn over and he runs a hand up my bare skin under my skirt, they are washed away by pure need.

Flipping my skirt up and baring me to his eyes brings a flush to my body. It seems ridiculous since he has already had his mouth on me there, but presenting myself seems even more intimate.

He makes a noise as his hands rub over the bared skin, trailing along my legs and over my ass cheeks and teasingly at the edge of my pussy. "So what you're showing me is that this whole time, including when we burned that asshole alive, you were walking around with no underwear and Rev's cum dripping from this pretty pussy?"

I'm about to respond when his hand cracks against my bare ass cheek. I'm not quick enough to stop the moan that escapes and his laugh is low and his voice is raspy. "You're so fucking perfect."

The door opening on the other side of the car in front of me is enough of a distraction that I don't pay attention to what Kai is doing until he is thrusting his cock inside of me to the hilt in one sharp movement. The force propels me forward, almost into Rev's lap as he slides in to sit on the back seat of the car in front of me, closing the car door behind him.

Obviously Kai doesn't care about anyone seeing his own ass with the limited street light and firelight close by because he leaves the door behind him wide open. Leaning over me he moves one of his feet to the footwell and lodges his knee between mine and the worn leather of the back seat.

This time when he thrusts into me harder he must be happier with the position because he digs his fingers into my hips and doesn't stop again. I'm gasping and moaning, my arms trembling as I try to keep myself upright even with the movement.

"Fuck, when I do die, I want it to be when I'm buried in this pussy."

I can feel him everywhere, his cock stretching me so good, just like his brother's did. I can feel every bump and ridge on his cock as it moves inside of me, his hip bones slapping so hard against my ass I wouldn't be surprised if I get bruises from that alone.

Rev fists a hand tightly in my hair, pulling my attention back to where he is sitting in front of me, his own cock now gripped in his tattooed hand.

"Wrap that hot mouth around me, baby girl."

He doesn't really need to tell me what to do. Leaning forward I use the momentum of one of Kai's thrusts to lick against the head of his cock above where his hand is. Then I swirl my tongue around him briefly on the next thrust. I make a frustrated sound when Kai pulls me back again and stops moving.

They both chuckle at me before Rev moves, changing his position so that he is turned toward me and leaning his upper back against the door. Now his cock is a lot closer. He uses the grip he has on my hair to tilt my head back until I'm where he wants me and then he is feeding me his hard cock.

I look up at Rev's face as I slowly swirl my tongue around the head of him again before closing my lips around him and taking as much of him in my mouth as I can. He is at the back of my throat when I choke around him briefly. I force myself to relax and take him even further, pushing past my limits. The groan that comes from him is the best fucking reward.

"I don't know what's better, your pussy or this fucking mouth. That's it, baby girl, fuck."

I breathe through my nose as I move my mouth up and down his length. Kai still doesn't move behind me yet, allowing me to take a moment. I grab Rev's other hand and move it to my hair beside the one already there.

He groans again when I swallow around him and squeeze his hand before putting my hand back on the seat for balance. "You want it hard, baby girl? You want me to take control?" His voice is husky, and I am so fucking on edge.

Kai grunts behind me, shifting his hips, his cock moving inside of me with the movement making me tighten around him more as he pulls back. "Fuck, yes she does. She likes that a lot. Don't you, gorgeous?"

I can only moan in response and the moment I do, Rev's hands twist in my hair as his hips jerk forward in response. Bites of pain pull at my scalp as he then pulls almost fully from my mouth.

He thrusts all the way back in, the head of his cock pushing down into my throat as I force it to stay relaxed and continue to breathe through my nose.

The next time he withdraws Kai slams his cock inside of me.

They set a primal, savage rhythm, one thrusting as the other withdraws. And I'm held between them with hard hands and tight fingers as they take complete control of my body.

I feel like I am exactly where I was always meant to be. I have never felt as much pleasure as I do at their hands.

It's not long before I'm riding the edge of release, my pussy tightening around Kai and the pressure building inside of me.

And then Kai stops.

I growl around Rev's cock, rocking my body back in an effort to chase him. But the vibration makes Rev twist his fists in my hair and push me down onto his cock, groaning deep and long as he jerks in my mouth. I swallow his cum greedily, momentarily forgetting my frustration.

Rev finally slumps back onto his heels, panting and mumbling under his breath about Kai being an asshole. Kai just laughs in response, knocking Rev's hands away from my hair to take a handful himself and pull me up and backward as far as the car would allow.

He lifts my leg and hooks it over the one he has bent and planted in the footwell, spreading me open wider.

My hands hit the roof and I cry out as Kai thrusts into me again. The angle is different, deeper and rubbing against different parts inside my pussy.

I'm not frustrated anymore. I'm in fucking ecstasy.

Kai reaches his free hand and starts circling my clit. "Tell me you have always wanted this, gorgeous. Tell me you have always secretly wanted our cocks like we wanted this pussy."

My moan is obscene. "Fuck, yesssss."

I'm not sure when my eyes fall closed but Rev's hand wraps around my throat moments before he breathes against my lips. "Keep those eyes open, baby girl. I love watching them shatter for us."

He doesn't kiss me, just holds me there as his brother keeps thrusting his cock hard and deep inside of me.

I moan again, my body tightening as the pressure keeps building. It's different and almost painful. "Godddddd."

Rev huffs a laugh against my lips. "I doubt he will help us after tonight, baby girl."

The pressure is too much, my body too tight. I can feel Kai struggling to keep thrusting. When he presses and rubs more firmly against my clit, my body shatters, my pussy pushing him out completely as liquid gushes from my pussy. His fingers keep rubbing hard across my clit back and forth as more liquid sprays across his cock and the leather car seat.

I can't catch my breath to scream. My mouth is wide open but no sound is coming out as waves of pleasure roll over me.

"Fuck yes," Kai moans before thrusting back into my pussy hard. I'm still coming down from that earth shattering moment when he grabs my hips again and starts pounding inside of me. It throws me straight into another smaller orgasm, my body clamping down on him once again, but this time taking him with me. His pace stutters as he groans deep in his chest.

The moment they groan out their release is now my new favorite sound. I want it on repeat.

I almost collapse onto the seat again, but Kai holds me up with a chuckle. Rev pulls off his jacket and then his shirt, using it to clean my dripping pussy before mopping up the mess we made on the seat. Once he's done, he throws the shirt into the footwell on his side and slides his jacket back on.

Kai releases me to take his own shirt off to clean himself and then puts his own jacket back on over his bare chest.

I think I'm drooling. They are dangerous to a woman's brain.

"You need to stop distracting me. I had a schedule and you keep blowing that and me out of the water."

Their laughter surrounds me and it's a light sound. Almost at odds with the purpose of the night. Even now, since our own sounds have died down there is no mistaking the sounds of chaos happening in other parts of the city streets. We were lucky to have avoided the chaos for as long as we have.

Rev runs a tattooed hand through his hair, clenching it in a fist, a habit he has when he is thinking. "Right, Silas."

I reach over and tug his hand from his hair, giving it a squeeze. "Ash said on that voice message that Silas is at the club tonight. He bought a nightclub about a month ago in the heart of the city and my guess is it will be one of the only places open all night tonight to celebrate Dead Devil's Night."

He frowns down at our joined hands as Kai leans over to kiss the back of my neck.

"So what was your plan?" Kai asks when Rev doesn't say anything.

"You need to trust me," I reply.

Both of their eyes narrow at me as almost identical frowns cross their faces.

"I'm going to get his attention. He prowls the club for what he wants... and he then takes it, willing or not. It shouldn't be too hard to catch his eye and then when we are alone, I will make my move. He has not counted on someone truly fighting back one day. And he will underestimate me."

Rev's frown deepens. "I'm not sure I will be able to stand by if he touches you."

As I go to say something, he looks at me with a savage look, his hand tightening on mine.

"You don't understand, I'm broken. I want to bathe in his blood for ever touching you. But I will try to control myself for you."

My heart thuds in my chest and I smile softly at him. "I think what happened last year broke something in all of us."

He is deep in thought for a moment before he gently lifts my hand and kisses the tops of my fingers. "We will be broken together, little bit. We will build a mosaic out of our broken and shattered pieces. We will make the world stare in awe at the masterpiece we create together."

Kai takes a hold of my other hand and also kisses it. "A masterpiece of death."

Chapter 13

RYLAN

The nightclub was appropriately named Devil's Lair. But on the streets it was called Hell.

And Hell is fucking pumping.

The seductive deep beats are playing loudly, I can feel the pulse of the music through my whole body. There is more people than I had planned for, especially given it is Dead Devil's Night, but I still had hope that my plan would work.

When we arrived and hid the car and bikes a street away, the twins almost had a fit when they remembered I still had nothing under my skirt. Luckily I came prepared. I pulled out some black leather booty shorts, which made them happy.

Until they also realized I still only have the mesh top on, which I wasn't going to change.

They had also devised their own plan to take out Silas, which involved them making their way to the rooftop access to get to the upper floor where Silas lived. It is the first time since we reunited where we aren't in eyesight of each other. And I hate it.

The security at the door meant that I couldn't bring my knives. All I could wear is my clothing and accessories as I walk into Hell. But I manage a few rings and necklaces that compliment my outfit.

There is people everywhere. The area had a large bar to the left and right side of the room with lounges and tables spread out surrounding a lowered dance floor called The Pit. There are stairs leading up to a mezzanine floor that hold another bar and all of the VIPs.

Moving through the bodies toward The Pit, I try to take it all in, taking peeks in all directions but never lingering. It only takes me a few moments to spot my target.

Silas Holt is surrounded by clingers and whores. But instead of paying attention to them, he is leaning against the railing watching The Pit and the writhing mass of bodies.

He has a black suit on, but the white shirt underneath is open halfway down his chest. It shows off the tattoos covering most of his skin and the thick gold chains that he is wearing to flaunt his wealth in a dead city. He is older than all the others, around his mid forties. His short black hair is slicked back on top and shaved at the sides and he has kept a thin layer of stubble on his face.

He might be attractive if he wasn't the epitome of Satan.

Focusing most of my attention back in front of me, I keep moving towards The Pit. If that's where he is looking, then that's where I need to be.

Pushing my way through the bodies, I find a spot toward the center, then I start moving to the beat. It doesn't take long to get into the rhythm, the thump of the base winding through my body as I dip and sway.

My hands snake up and into my hair, gripping it and giving it a shake before I raise them high. Moving them back down my body, I touch every part of me on the way back down, pulling my jacket just off my shoulders to give anyone above me a teasing view through the mesh of my top.

Throwing my head back, I close my eyes and part my lips like I'm in ecstasy just from the act of moving to the beat. My hands continue to move over my body, touching everywhere. If I didn't have a date with the devil, then the music and movement might have actually turned me on.

I feel hands on my hips and when I open my eyes a fraction, I can see that I have the devil's attention. Turning toward the hands that are touching me, I silently hope that the twins do not have a view of me from wherever they are, otherwise this poor unfortunate sap may not survive the night either. Dismissing any potential concern, I step into the body, draping my arms over the broad shoulders and allowing him to wedge a knee between my legs as we start grinding on each other.

The guy is relatively attractive in a boy next door sort of way. Wavy light brown hair, lightly tanned skin and a bright smile. I'm sure he thinks he is lucky at this moment, the poor misguided fool.

It doesn't take long. We are only dancing together for a few short minutes before someone appears beside us out of the mass of bodies, his fingers tapping my shoulder lightly.

I start to dismiss him as though I have no interest in him, but he leans closer to my ear to shout over the music. "Mr. Holt would like you to join him."

Looking back toward the man, I raise a brow and he points to where Silas is leaning against the railing still. He has a smirk on his face, so I play along and smile sweetly back.

Turning back to my dance partner, I lean in briefly, my lips almost brushing his ear. "Thank you for the dance. Me leaving is you getting lucky. Find a sweet girl to take home instead."

Letting him go, I move to follow the hired muscle and don't give the boy another thought. He is a means to an end.

I'm led to a private elevator at the back of the club and directed in through the open doors. Instead of getting on with me, the man just turns to stand guard in front of it as the doors slide closed, trapping me inside of it alone. It's slow to start moving, but then starts ascending toward the mezzanine floor. When the doors finally open, the Devil is waiting.

Silas is standing directly in front of the open elevator doors and instead of allowing me to step off, he steps on and presses the button to take us to the top of the building. The smirk is still on his face, and all I want to do is wipe it off.

Taking a few steps to close the distance, he braces his hands on the elevator wall on either side of my body. "Hey there, sweetheart."

I give a coy smile and look up at him through my lashes. "Hi. Where are we going?"

He snickers, moving a hand to drag a finger down the side of my face and I suppress a shudder. "A private party. Just you and me."

I hum and force myself to lean my face toward the hand touching me, playing along.

"You'd like that, wouldn't you, sweetheart? To party just with me."

I nod in response and I don't even need to fake that enthusiasm, because really, I do want to party just with him. And his blood as I slice him wide open.

His smirk gets even wider as the elevator slows to a stop, the doors opening slowly behind him. He turns and slides a hand behind my back, pressing against it and not so subtly pushing me out of the elevator and into his apartment.

The place is luxe, and I admit it is beautiful. The main feature is the wall of glass that gives the perfect view of the chaos outside. The fires can be seen all over the city and I wonder if this would have given a good view of the fire we made when we burned Ash alive.

Everything in the apartment is darkness and shadows, the only light coming from above the elevator. When I look back toward the only light source, it illuminates Silas standing there behind me.

With a gun aimed in my direction. Still wearing that insufferable smirk.

"You didn't truly think I wouldn't recognize you the moment you stepped into my club, right?"

RYLAN

Well, it is official, the twins are going to hunt me in hell and kill my ass again for telling them to trust me.

Trying not to show anything apart from humor, I smirk back at the asshole. "It was the hair, wasn't it?" I laugh and use a hand to flick some of it over my shoulder. "What can I say, I was feeling nostalgic."

His eyes narrow slightly and I can see the smirk become a little strained around the edges at me not cowering before him. I am pushing my luck, really, but I am never going to cower and cry in front of this man ever again.

Tilting his head, he looks me over, probably trying to see if I have any weapons on me. I wish I had another one of my handy rings, but even if I did and was able to sneak it past security, judging from the gun, he never would have let me lay a hand on him.

"So what exactly was your plan, sweetheart? Sneak in and kill me in revenge?" There is humor in his voice and it grates on my nerves.

I laugh, because seriously, did he really want me to just come out and say yes, I came with the intent of killing him? Fuck that. "Do I look like I'm sneaking anywhere? I was simply dancing. It was you who dragged me up here."

Turning around, I look around the apartment again. It was a proverbial 'fuck you' to dismiss him like that, but I know he wasn't about to shoot me in the back. Simply by being there last year, he proved he liked a more personal touch with his maiming and killing.

The furniture is black and dark wood. The apartment is large, with an open plan living and dining area and a buffet style kitchen along one section of wall. I could just make out doorways in the darkness leading off both sides of the room, which I assumed led to bedrooms.

Stepping off the elevator landing, I walk toward the glass, watching in the reflection as Silas follows the movement. He slowly steps down after me, but doesn't follow me too closely. He keeps his distance, staying close to the landing while still keeping within shooting range. The frown on his face tells me I'm not acting the way he wants me to act, like I care what he wants.

"How the fuck are you still alive? I thought I had done a pretty good job of killing you."

I grin at him over my shoulder. "Dead Devil's Night seems to be my lucky night."

I can see amusement cross his face again and his eyes run over me again condescendingly. "So you thought you could get lucky again this year and get revenge? Sounds like the stupid idea of a crazy girl."

Humming, I turn around to face him again with a genuine grin of my own. He is still steadily aiming the gun at me. "Maybe crazy, but my luck seems to be holding out so far."

The amusement becomes strained on his face again, and I can almost see the cogs turning inside his mind as he tries to understand what I'm getting at. He keeps the gun steady as he reaches into the pocket of his jacket and extracts his phone.

I watch with my amusement growing as he tries number after number with no answer. After the last one, he growls in frustration and throws the phone across the room to be lost in the darkness.

Narrowing his eyes at me again, his face loses all the humor and amusement that he once wore. His eyes almost glitter with malice. "No great loss, I can easily replace them. I suppose you think you're something special for killing them."

"I don't know about me being special, but their deaths definitely were. Would you like to hear about them? I know you love chaos, so I'm sure you will enjoy hearing all about it."

He doesn't respond, so I continue as though he has agreed with me. I wanted him to hear all about it, to understand the joy I felt with every one of them. And I want him to imagine me doing the same to him.

I start slowly pacing in front of the window. "Let's see, Karver was first. You know he likes his whores right? He likes them on the sweet and innocent looking side." I pause and bring my hands under my chin and give him a fluttering of my lashes. "It wasn't hard to get his attention. Then it wasn't hard to paralyze him and start cutting him up. He didn't last long after I cut his dick off and slit his throat."

There is a microscopic flinch to his eyes. A purely male response.

I grin savagely but keep pacing. "Then there was Damien. He likes the girls too, but he prefers the ones that are going to supply his habit." I tap a finger to my nose so he doesn't mistake what habit I'm talking about. "Flash a little skin and a little plastic bag and he was practically drooling for me. It's a shame that it was a dirty batch with more chemicals than cocaine. His veins turned a pretty shade of black before he choked on his own blood."

If I didn't know better, I would have thought Silas looked a little green with that one. It made me wonder if he liked the white stuff too.

"Kasen was next. But I'm sure you can guess the order by now right? Kasen took a little more planning. He didn't like whores or drugs, but he did like to pick up a bottle of bourbon each day and took the same path back to his apartment. You really should have taught them not to be so predictable. He didn't even see the bear trap before he stepped in it. And then when the chains pulled him up into the air, all I needed to do was cut him up. I did get to stab him in the dick also before he was beaten to death with a bat."

I don't mention that I wasn't the one to beat him to death. He still needs to think the boys are dead.

"I almost didn't catch Ash, though. By the time I got to his apartment, someone had already called him about Karver. I thought I was going to have to trudge all the way back to the whorehouse to get him. But as I said, luck seems to be in my favor tonight and he had to change his tire first. I don't imagine he enjoyed being burnt alive when I set his car on fire with him inside."

Turning back toward Silas I stop pacing, resting my hands on my hips. I can see that he thinks I'm utterly crazy, and yeah, I probably am, but in the end he did contribute to my madness.

"Which brings me to you."

He tilts his head again with a frown. "Maybe I should have recruited you instead."

I raise an eyebrow at that. "Was that before or after you raped me and tried to murder me?"

He scoffs, and a grin returns to his face. "You think I went into that night blind? I had already done my research. I knew who you were before I even entered that apartment. Poor little orphan girl, no one was going to miss you."

The confession doesn't surprise me. I had already worked that part out. I knew more than he thought I did. "And you think I've come into tonight blind? I've done my research too. Tell me, how did it feel killing your own sons that night?"

RYLAN

H is grin doesn't even falter. If anything, it gets bigger, the sadistic fuck.

And still the gun doesn't waver.

"Pretty and smart. I definitely should have recruited you. Maybe then you might be on the end of my dick instead of my gun."

I can't stop the disgusted cringe that crosses my face as I look at him. "Eww, no. And for the record, your sons fucked me better."

The grin finally disappears from his face as fury takes over. Men are so predictable, insult their manhood and they take it so personally. He takes a step closer to me and adjusts his grip, I can see that he is itching to pull the trigger now.

"Such a shame I took your boy toys away from you then," he sneered at me.

I let the slow smile spread across my lips. "I wouldn't be so sure about that."

The sound of the bat hitting the side of his head was almost better than the sound of my guys groaning their climaxes. Almost.

Silas is far too arrogant and self assured, so he never once checked his surroundings when he exited the elevator. He thought he had the upper hand, but he never did. I felt them the moment I stepped into the apartment. They were so ingrained in my soul that just their proximity was calming.

The sound of the gun going off is loud in the room, but thankfully, it doesn't hit anything important. The gun ends up sliding across the smooth floor and out of Silas' reach.

He isn't down though, and even with the spikes of the bat tearing into the flesh at the side of his head, he still stays standing. He turns toward his attacker with a snarl, only to get a heavy boot to the chest that finally sends him crashing to the floor.

Kai swings the bat again with a grin, landing the shot in the middle of Silas' back and drawing a shout from the sadistic fuck's mouth. And just for good measure, Kai then drags the barbs downward before pulling the bat away and letting Rev press a heavy boot where the spikes were only moments before.

It doesn't take long for Kai to drag over a chair and for them to secure Silas into it, tying his arms and legs so tightly it wouldn't surprise me if he no longer had blood flow to them.

Ignoring the snarling and cursing coming from Silas, Rev closes the distance with me, cradling my face and kissing me deeply. "I'm totally spanking that ass for that whole 'trust me' shit."

Chuckling, I brush my lips across his again. "Don't threaten me with a good time."

Turning back toward Silas, I take in the grinning Kai standing guard next to him. I can't help running my eyes over him. He shoots me a wink and reaches for something behind his back. "We brought you presents."

He's holding out my two knives, and I practically skip across the floor to take them from his hands. Once his hands are empty, he drags my lips to his in a savage kiss that tells me that the momentary distance aggravated him as much as it did me.

I grin at him when he finally releases me. "Remind me to thank you properly later."

He laughs and just picks up his bat again from where he dropped it to secure Silas.

The twins take up positions beside me as I look at Silas. Blood is dripping down the side of his face where Kai first hit him, and I can see the edge of pain that he is trying to hide behind a sneer. His eyes are looking back and forth between Rev and Kai.

"I should have hunted you down harder when that junkie cunt told me she hid you away."

Rev doesn't even need to move forward much before swinging his bat down and landing a hit to Silas' knee. This time Silas just grunts and grits his teeth, trying to portray the tough man he really isn't.

But he can't hide the flash of pain in his eyes, and I revel in it.

I chuckle again. "Well, I'm glad she did. The home she hid them in was how I met them. The biggest mistake you made was attacking me."

This time he laughs. "It was never about you. You were just a pathetic little cunt that they were obsessed with. A means to an end, a way to make them suffer. When I finally found them, I was going to let them go, but then they thought they could try to take over my territory."

Still, none of this comes as a surprise to me. This time it's Kai's bat that lands on Silas' other knee and Silas screws his face up and closes his eyes against the pain.

Stepping forward, I lean into his space. "So, how did that work out for you, hmm?" Slowly I push the knives in my hands into the flesh of his thighs and he gives a long and pained groan.

His eyes flash to mine as I drag the knives back out of his legs. "You won't get away with this, you little bitch. I'm not the top of the food chain here. You won't get away with killing me."

I give him a surprised and worried look, holding a blood flecked hand in front of my face. "Really?" My voice trembles for a second before I laugh at him again. "And when was the last time you spoke to your boss, like actually spoke on the phone with him?"

He frowns; mixed with the pain, it's an almost comical look. I could almost see the cogs turning slowly.

"I'd say it was about a month ago, right?" I ask. "Just before he was shot in a liquor store holdup close to our house."

All emotion vanishes from Silas' face.

"He told you to leave the twins alone, and then you didn't follow his orders. That was why he was even there that night and rescued me. I asked him why he left you alive, and he said that your death was no longer his to take."

The fear is finally in Silas' eyes, and the sight is better than anything else I have seen so far that night.

"So, for the past year, he helped me plot and plan my revenge. And while you licked his boots like a good little boy hoping for scraps to work your way into his legacy, he taught me how to rule."

I smile fondly at the memories. "He taught me everything, including patience. Like that old saying, the one about revenge being a dish best served cold. Is this cold enough for you?"

Pushing the knives into his groin, I finally get the scream I am waiting for. Pulling the knives back out, I can see the blood spreading faster now.

"You never knew who he really was, you just followed orders like a good soldier. I mean, David's disguise was genius, who would ever suspect an old beat cop of running a criminal empire? But I like our new disguise better. Thanks to you, the world thinks we are dead."

Stepping back to the twins, I hold a knife out to each of them with a grin. "I believe these have your names on them. This death belongs to you, too."

Kai flashes me a savage grin, taking the knife on his side and moving past me. Rev takes the knife but lays a kiss against my head and murmurs into my ear before following Kai. "So fucking perfect."

I don't bother watching. Silas' final moments no longer interest me. He doesn't deserve the extra attention.

It doesn't take long for Silas to take his last breath, and I know the twins probably made it quick in order to be sure there was no chance of Silas surviving like we had. They learned the lesson that Silas thankfully hadn't.

Turning my back on the view of the city once again, I wave my hands out the windows as though I'm a sales girl. "Welcome to our empire, boys."

Kai gives an exaggerated bow. "My beautiful Empress."

I'm suddenly in his arms as he swings me around in the air, making me giggle like I did growing up with them.

Rev reaches out once I'm back on my feet and tucks my hair behind my ear. "So what does this mean?"

I laugh joyously. I know he wants to know about who I became over the last year, but I just couldn't bring myself to discuss it that night. It had been a long night. Well, a long year, really. "Well, I believe it means you just inherited a nightclub. It's so good too! Wanna go dance?"

Not taking no for an answer, I move past them and over to the elevator. Throwing a smirk over my shoulder at them, I pull off my leather jacket and throw it to the side, fully intent on distracting them and having some fun to celebrate. "Someone was getting handsy earlier, so you may have competition."

I squeal and give a hysterical laugh when Rev picks me up and throws me over his shoulder before stepping into the open elevator. His hand cracks loudly across my ass cheek.

Kai cackles and steps onto the elevator beside me. "No such thing, gorgeous girl."

I grin. Best night ever.

Author's Note

I hope you enjoyed Dead Devil's Night!

Thank you to my husband for always answering my weird and dark questions and picking your brain for all the good crime/forensic/chemical etc information.

As always thank you to my team of amazing alpha and beta readers, especially for pretty much reading this at the drop of a hat when I threw it at you in the 11th hour.

Thank you to my Street and ARC team for being great spokespeople for a relatively unknown indie author.

And thank you to my readers for picking up this book and supporting me, I appreciate you.

xx

Maree Rose

About the Author

Maree is a indie author who although she has been writing most of her life, never thought she would ever get something published, which is now why she published this herself. She has always been an avid reader since a young age after roaming through book exchanges with her mum when she was just starting to read serious big girl books.

Maree lives on the East Coast of Australia with her wonderful husband, her son and her two gorgeous squishy british bulldogs.

When she is not writing she is working in a financial career (for something completely different to the creative side) or she is working on her photography (which is just as hot as her books).

Stalk Me

Please feel free to stalk me.

Like metaphorically, not literally of course!

Facebook:

Follow My Page

Join My Readers Group

Make sure you join my Reader Group for bonus scenes and extra content!

Amazon:

Follow My Author Page

Goodreads:

Follow My Profile

SHATTERED WORLD

Shattered Safety Duet:
Untouchable & Unbreakable
Shattered Memories Duet:
Unforgettable & Unstoppable (COMING SOON)

THE MASQUERADE

Make Me Learn

DARLING WORLD

hunt me darling

hide me darling (COMING SOON)